DISNEY · PIXAR

INSIDE OUT

SADNESS

by **Brittany Candau**
illustrated by **Jerrod Maruyama**

DISNEY PRESS

Los Angeles · New York

Sigh.

Hi, I'm

Sadness.

I usually feel pretty **blue**.

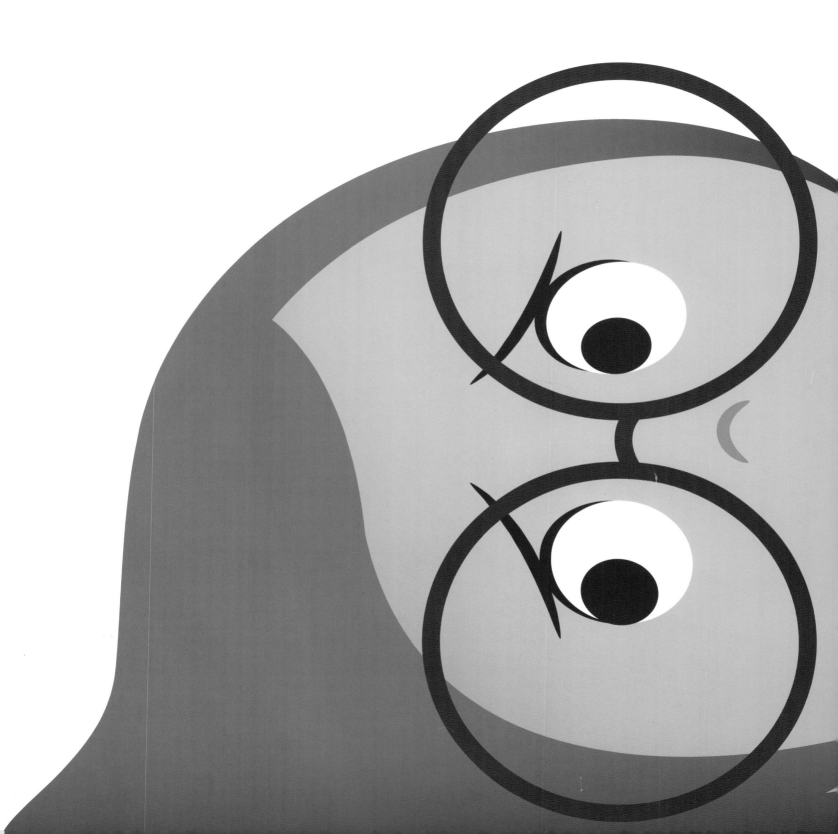

I just don't understand the world sometimes.

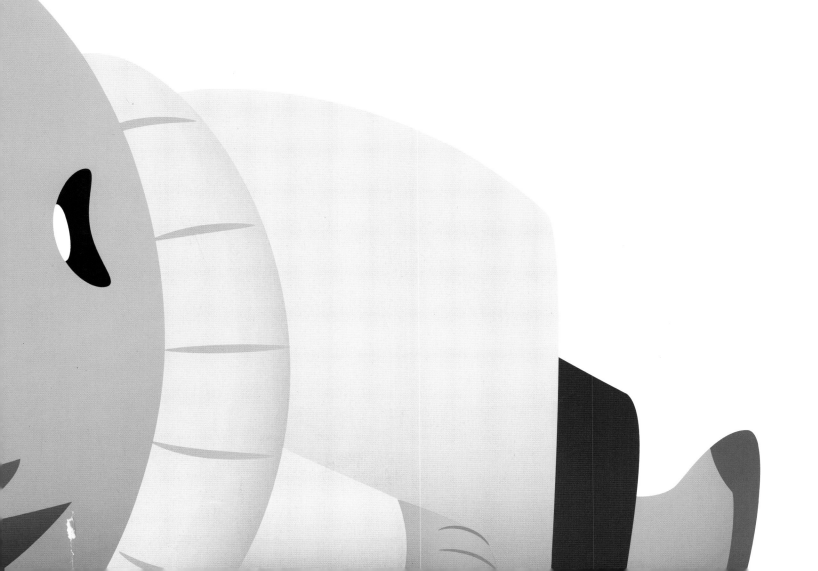

Like why does ice cream **fall off** the cone?

Or why do

My balloon has popped.

My night-light has stopped working.

It is a dark day

pencils break?

I like

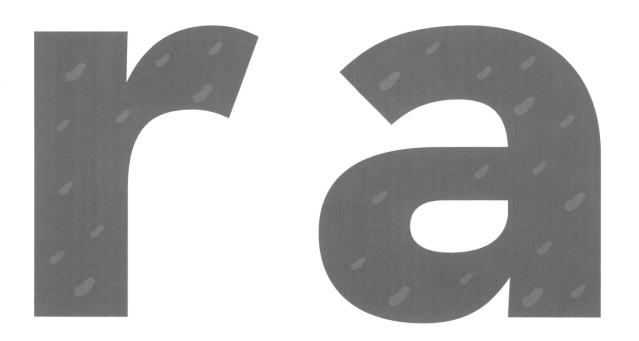

r a

It makes you

in.

shivery and droopy.

Puppies can be cute. But then they chew on your new sweater.

Things just move too fast nowadays.

I always seem to

lose

something.

Or I'm the one who's **lost.**

I like crying.

It helps me slow down and obsess over the weight of life's problems.

And I feel better.

But then I feel **sad** again.

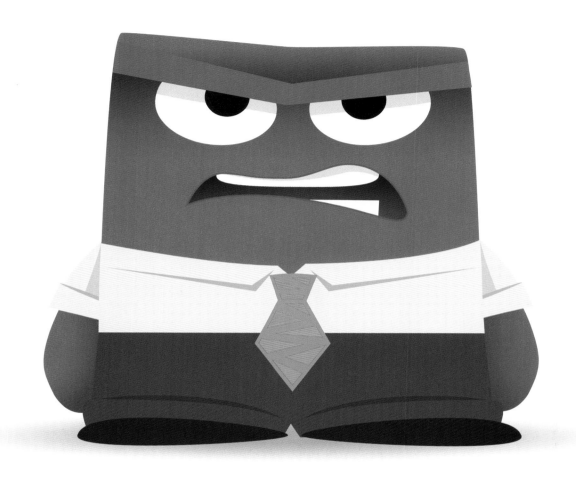

You have GOT to
be kidding me!